MW00377885

LOVE LETTERS OF GREAT MEN:

The Collection of Love Letters Drawn from by Carrie Bradshaw in "Sex in the City"

Contents

JOHN ADAMS

to Abigail Adams

Octr. 4th. 1762

Miss Adorable

By the same Token that the Bearer hereof *satt up* with you last night I hereby order you to give him, as many Kisses, and as many Hours of your Company after 9 O'Clock as he shall please to Demand and charge them to my Account: This Order, or Requisition call it which you will is in Consideration of a similar order Upon Aurelia for the like favour, and I presume I have good Right to draw upon you for the Kisses as I have given two or three Millions at least, when one has been received, and of Consequence the Account between us is immensely in favour of yours,

John Adams

Philadelphia July 7. 1775

My Dear

I have received your very agreable Favours of June 22d. and 25th. They contain more particulars than any Letters I had before received from any Body.

It is not at all surprizing to me that the wanton, cruel, and infamous Conflagration of Charlestown, the Place of your Fathers Nativity, should afflict him. Let him know that I sincerely condole with him, on that mellancholly Event. It is a Method of conducting War long since become disreputable among civilized Nations: But every Year brings us fresh Evidence, that We have nothing to hope for from our loving Mother Country, but Cruelties more abominable than those which are practiced by the Savage Indians.

The account you give me of the Numbers slain on the side of our Enemies, is affecting to Humanity, altho it is a glorious Proof of the Bravery of our Worthy Countrymen. Considering all the Disadvantages under which they fought, they really exhibited Prodigies of Valour.

Your Description of the Distresses of the worthy Inhabitants of Boston, and the other Sea Port Towns, is enough to melt an Heart of stone. Our Consolation must be this, my dear, that Cities may be rebuilt, and a People reduced to Poverty, may acquire fresh Property: But a Constitution of Government once changed from Freedom, can never be restored. Liberty once lost is lost forever. When the People once surrender their share in the Legislature, and their Right of defending the Limitations upon the Government, and of resisting every Encroachment upon them, they can never regain it.

The Loss of Mr. Mathers Library, which was a Collection, of Books and Manuscripts made by himself, his Father, his Grandfather, and Greatgrandfather, and was really very curious and valuable, is irreparable.

The Family picture you draw is charming indeed. My dear Nabby, Johnny, Charly and Tommy, I long to see you, and to share with your Mamma the Pleasures of your Conversation.

I feel myself much obliged to Mr. Bowdoin, Mr. Wibirt, and the two Families you mention, for their Civilities to you. My Compli· ments to them. Does Mr. Wibirt preach against Oppression, and the other Cardinal Vices of the Times? Tell him the Clergy here, of every Denomination, not excepting the Episcopalian, thunder and lighten every sabbath. They pray for Boston and the Massachusetts—they thank God most explicitly and fervently for our remarkable Successes—they pray for the American Army. They seem to feel as if they were among you.

You ask if every Member feels for Us? Every Member says he does—and most of them really do. But most of them feel more for themselves. In every Society of Men, in every Clubb, I ever yet saw, you find some who are timid, their Fears hurry them away upon every Alarm—some who are selfish and avaricious, on whose callous Hearts nothing but Interest and Money can make Impression. There are some Persons in New York and Philadelphia, to whom a ship is dearer than a City, and a few Barrells of flower, than a thousand Lives—other Mens Lives I mean.

You ask, can they reallize what We suffer? I answer No. They cant, they dont—and to excuse them as well as I can, I must confess I should not be able to do it, myself, if I was not more acquainted with it by Experience than they are.

I am grieved for Dr. Tufts's ill Health: but rejoiced exceedingly at his virtuous Exertions in the Cause of his Country.

I am happy to hear that my Brothers were at Grape Island and behaved well. My Love to them, and Duty to my Mother.

It gives me more Pleasure than I can express to learn that you sustain with so much Fortitude, the Shocks and Terrors of the

Times. You are really brave, my dear, you are an Heroine. And you have Reason to be. For the worst that can happen, can do you no Harm. A soul, as pure, as benevolent, as virtuous and pious as yours has nothing to fear, but every Thing to hope and expect from the last of human Evils. Am glad you have secured an Assylum, tho I hope you will not have occasion for it.

Love to Brother Cranch and sister and the Children.

There is an amiable, ingenious Hussy, named Betcy Smith, for whom I have a very great Regard. Be pleased to make my Love acceptable to her, and let her know, that her elegant Pen cannot be more usefully employed than in Writing Letters to her Brother at Phyladelphia, tho it may more agreably in writing Billet doux to young Gentlemen.

The other Day, after I had received a Letter of yours, with one or two others, Mr. William Barrell desired to read them. I put them into his Hand, and the next Morning had them returned in a large Bundle packed up with two great Heaps of Pins, with a very polite Card requesting Portias Acceptance of them. I shall bring them with me I return: But when that will be is uncertain.—I hope not more than a Month hence.

I have really had a very disagreable Time of it. My Health and especialy my Eyes have been so very bad, that I have not been so fit for Business as I ought, and if I had been in perfect Health, I should have had in the present Condition of my Country and my Friends, no Taste for Pleasure. But Dr. Young has made a kind of Cure of my Health and Dr. Church of my Eyes. Have received two kind Letters from your Unkle Smith—do thank him for them—I shall forever love him for them. I love every Body that writes to me.

I am forever yours—

SULLIVAN BALLOU

to Sarah Hart Shumway

July the 14th, 1861

Washington D.C.

My very dear Sarah:

The indications are very strong that we shall move in a few days—perhaps tomorrow. Lest I should not be able to write you again, I feel impelled to write lines that may fall under your eye when I shall be no more.

Our movement may be one of a few days duration and full of pleasure—and it may be one of severe conflict and death to me. Not my will, but thine O God, be done. If it is necessary that I should fall on the battlefield for my country, I am ready. I have no misgivings about, or lack of confidence in, the cause in which I am engaged, and my courage does not halt or falter. I know how strongly American Civilization now leans upon the triumph of the Government, and how great a debt we owe to those who went before us through the blood and suffering of the Revolution. And I am willing—perfectly willing—to lay down all my joys in this life, to help maintain this Government, and to pay that debt.

But, my dear wife, when I know that with my own joys I lay down nearly all of yours, and replace them in this life with cares and sorrows—when, after having eaten for long years the bitter fruit of orphanage myself, I must offer it as their only sustenance to my dear little children—is it weak or dishonorable, while the banner of my purpose floats calmly and proudly in the breeze, that my unbounded love for you, my darling wife and children, should struggle in fierce, though useless, contest with my love of country.

Sarah, my love for you is deathless, it seems to bind me to you with mighty cables that nothing but Omnipotence could break; and yet my love of Country comes over me like a strong wind and bears me irresistibly on with all these chains to the battlefield.

The memories of the blissful moments I have spent with you come creeping over me, and I feel most gratified to God and to you that I have enjoyed them so long. And hard it is for me to give them up and burn to ashes the hopes of future years, when God willing, we might still have lived and loved together and seen our sons grow up to honorable manhood around us. I have, I know, but few and small claims upon Divine Providence, but something whispers to me—perhaps it is the wafted prayer of my little Edgar—that I shall return to my loved ones unharmed. If I do not, my dear Sarah, never forget how much I love you, and when my last breath escapes me on the battlefield, it will whisper your name.

Forgive my many faults, and the many pains I have caused you. How thoughtless and foolish I have often been! How gladly would I wash out with my tears every little spot upon your happiness, and struggle with all the misfortune of this world, to shield you and my children from harm. But I cannot. I must watch you from the spirit land and hover near you, while you buffet the storms with your precious little freight, and wait with sad patience till we meet to part no more.

But, O Sarah! If the dead can come back to this earth and flit unseen around those they loved, I shall always be near you; in the brightest day and in the darkest night—amidst your happiest scenes and gloomiest hours—always, always; and if there be a soft breeze upon your cheek, it shall be my breath; or the cool air fans your throbbing temple, it shall be my spirit passing by.

Sarah, do not mourn me dead; think I am gone and wait for me, for we shall meet again.

As for my little boys, they will grow as I have done, and never know a father's love and care. Little Willie is too young to remember me long, and my blue-eyed Edgar will keep my frolics with him among the dimmest memories of his childhood. Sarah, I have unlimited confidence in your maternal care and your development of their characters. Tell my two mothers his and hers I call God's blessing upon them. O Sarah, I wait for you there! Come to me, and lead thither my children.

Sullivan

LOVE LETTERS OF GREAT MEN: THE COLLECTION OF LOVE LETTERS
DRAWN FROM BY CARRIE BRADSHAW IN "SEX IN THE CITY"

HONORE DE BALZAC

to Ewelina Hanska

June 1835

MY BELOVED ANGEL,

I am nearly mad about you, as much as one can be mad: I cannot bring together two ideas that you do not interpose yourself between them. I can no longer think of nothing but you. In spite of myself, my imagination carries me to you. I grasp you, I kiss you, I caress you, a thousand of the most amorous caresses take possession of me. As for my heart, there you will always be — very much so. I have a delicious sense of you there. But my God, what is to become of me, if you have deprived me of my reason? This is a monomania which, this morning, terrifies me. I rise up every moment say to myself, 'Come, I am going there!' Then I sit down again, moved by the sense of my obligations. There is a frightful conflict. This is not a life. I have never before been like that. You have devoured everything. I feel foolish and happy as soon as I let myself think of you. I whirl round in a delicious dream in which in one instant I live a thousand years. What a horrible situation! Overcome with love, feeling love in every pore, living only for love, and seeing oneself consumed by griefs, and caught in a thousand spiders' threads. O, my darling Eva, you did not know it. I picked up your card. It is there before me, and I talked to you as if you were here. I see you, as I did yesterday, beautiful, astonishingly beautiful. Yesterday, during the whole evening, I said to myself 'She is mine!' Ah! The angels are not as happy in Paradise as I was yesterday!

LOVE LETTERS OF GREAT MEN: THE COLLECTION OF LOVE LETTERS
DRAWN FROM BY CARRIE BRADSHAW IN "SEX IN THE CITY"

LUDVIG VON BEETHOVEN

to an unknown lover

6 July, morning

My angel, my all, my own self — only a few words today, and that too with pencil (with yours) — only till tomorrow is my lodging definitely fixed. What abominable waste of time in such things — why this deep grief, where necessity speaks? Can our love persist otherwise than through sacrifices, than by not demanding everything? Canst thou change it, that thou are not entirely mine, I not entirely thine? Oh, God, look into beautiful Nature and compose your mind to the inevitable. Love demands everything and is quite right, so it is for me with you, for you with me — only you forget so easily, that I must live for you and for me — were we quite united, you would notice this painful feeling as little as I should . . .

. . . We shall probably soon meet, even today I cannot communicate my remarks to you, which during these days I made about my life — were our hearts close together, I should probably not make any such remarks. My bosom is full, to tell you much — there are moments when I find that speech is nothing at all. Brighten up — remain my true and only treasure, my all, as I to you. The rest the gods must send, what must be for us and shall.

Your faithful

Ludwig

Monday evening, 6 July

You suffer, you, my dearest creature. Just now I perceive that letters must be posted first thing early. Mondays – Thursdays – the only days, when the post goes from here to K. You suffer – oh! Where I am, you are with me, with me and you, I shall arrange that I may live with you. What a life!

So! Without you – pursued by the kindness of the people here and there, whom I mean – to desire to earn just as little as they earn – humility of man towards men – it pains me – and when I regard myself in connection with the Universe, what I am, and what he is – whom one calls the greatest – and yet – there lies herein again the godlike of man. I weep when I think you will probably only receive on Saturday the first news from me – as you too love – yet I love you stronger – but never hide yourself from me. Good night – as I am taking the waters, I must go to bed. Oh God – so near! so far! Is it not a real building of heaven, our Love – but as firm, too, as the citadel of heaven.

Good morning, on 7 July

Even in bed my ideas yearn towards you, my Immortal Beloved, here and there joyfully, then again sadly, awaiting from Fate, whether it will listen to us. I can only live, either altogether with you or not at all. Yes, I have determined to wander about for so long far away, until I can fly into your arms and call myself quite at home with you, can send my soul enveloped by yours into the realm of spirits – yes, I regret, it must be. You will get over it all the more as you know my faithfulness to you; never another one can own my heart, never – never! O God, why must one go away from what one loves so, and yet my life in W. as it is now is a miserable life. Your love made me the happiest and unhappiest at the same time. At my actual age I should need some continuity, sameness of life – can that exist under our circumstances? Angel, I just hear that the post goes out every day – and must close therefore, so that you get the L. at once. Be calm – love me – today – yesterday.

What longing in tears for you — You — my Life — my All — farewell. Oh, go on loving me — never doubt the faithfullest heart

Of your beloved

L

Ever thine.

Ever mine.

Ever ours.

NAPOLEAN BONAPARTE

to Josephine Bonaparte

I have not spent a day without loving you; I have not spent a night without embracing you; I have not so much as drunk a single cup of tea without cursing the pride and ambition which force me to remain separated from the moving spirit of my life.

In the midst of my duties, whether I am at the head of my army or inspecting the camps, my beloved Josephine stands alone in my heart, occupies my mind, fills my thoughts. If I am moving away from you with the speed of the Rhone torrent, it is only that I may see you again more quickly.

If I rise to work in the middle of the night, it is because this may hasten by a matter of days the arrival of my sweet love. Yet in your letter of the 23rd, and 26th. Ventose, you call me vous. Vous yourself!

Ah! wretch, how could you have written this letter? How cold it is? And then there are those four days between the 23rd, and the 26th.; what were you doing that you failed to write to your husband? ... Ah, my love, that vous, those four days made me long for my former indifference. Woe to the person responsible!

May he as punishment and penalty, experience what my convictions and the evidence (which is in your friend's favor) would make me experience!

Hell has no torments great enough! Nor do the Furies have serpents enough! Vous! Vous!

Ah! how will things stand in two weeks? ... My spirit is heavy; my heart is fettered and I am terrified by my fantasies... You love me less; but you will get over the loss. One day you will love me no longer; at least tell me; then I shall know how I have come to deserve this misfortune. ...Farewell, my wife: the torment, joy, hope and moving which draw me close to Nature, and with violent impulses as tumultuous as thunder. I ask of you neither eternal love, nor fidelity, but simply...truth, unlimited honesty.

The day when you say "I love you less", will mark the end of my love and the last day of my life. If my heart were base enough to love without being loved in return I would tear it to pieces.

Josephine! Josephine! Remember what I have sometimes said to you: Nature has endowed me with a virile and decisive character. It has built yours out of lace and gossamer. Have you ceased to love me? Forgive me, love of my life, my soul is racked by conflicting forces. My heart obsessed by you, is full of fears which prostrate me with misery...I am distressed not to be calling you by name. I shall wait for you to write it.

Farewell! Ah! if you love me less you can never have loved me. In that case I shall truly be pitiable.

Bonaparte

P.S. The war this year has changed beyond recognition. I have had meat, bread and fodder distributed; my armed cavalry will soon be on the march. My soldiers are showing inexpressible confidence in me; you alone are a source of chagrin to me; you alone are the joy and torment of my life. I send a kiss to your children, whom you do not mention. By God! If you did, your letters would be half as long again. Then visitors at ten o'clock in the morning would not have the pleasure of seeing you. Woman!!!

ROBERT BROWNING

to Elizabeth Browning

January 10th, 1845

New Cross, Hatcham, Surrey

I love your verses with all my heart, dear Miss Barrett,--and this is no off-hand complimentary letter that I shall write,--whatever else, no prompt matter-of-course recognition of your genius and there a graceful and natural end of the thing: since the day last week when I first read your poems, I quite laugh to remember how I have been turning again in my mind what I should be able to tell you of their effect upon me--for in the first flush of delight I though I would this once get out of my habit of purely passive enjoyment, when I do really enjoy, and thoroughly justify my admiration--perhaps even, as a loyal fellow-craftsman should, try and find fault and do you some little good to be proud of herafter!--but nothing comes of it all--so into me has it gone, and part of me has it become, this great living poetry of yours, not a flower of which but took root and grew... oh, how different that is from lying to be dried and pressed flat and prized highly and put in a book with a proper account at bottom, and shut up and put away... and the book called a 'Flora', besides! After all, I need not give up the thought of doing that, too, in time; because even now, talking with whoever is worthy, I can give reason for my faith in one and another excellence, the fresh strange music, the affluent language, the exquisite pathos and true new brave thought--but in this addressing myself to you, your own self, and for the first time, my feeling rises altogher. I do, as I say, love these Books with all my heart-- and I love you too: do you know

I was once seeing you? Mr. Kenyon said to me one morning "would you like to see Miss Barrett?"--then he went to announce me,--then he returned... you were too unwell -- and now it is years ago--and I feel as at some untoward passage in my travels--as if I had been close, so close, to some world's-wonder in chapel on crypt,... only a screen to push and I might have entered -- but there was some slight... so it now seems... slight and just-sufficient bar to admission, and the half-opened door shut, and I went home my thousands of miles, and the sight was never to be!

Well, these Poems were to be--and this true thankful joy and pride with which I feel myself. Yours ever faithfully Robert Browning

ROBERT BURNS

to Agnes MeLehose

I

Clarinda, my life, you have wounded my soul.-Can I think of your being unhappy, even tho' it be not described in your pathetic elegance of language, without being miserable?

Clarinda, can I bear to be told from you, that "you will not see me tomorrow night-that you wish the hour of parting were come"! Do not let us impose on ourselves by sounds: if in the moment of fond endearment and tender dalliance, I perhaps trespassed against the letter of Decorum's law; I appeal, even to you, wbether I ever smned m the very least degree against the spirit of her strictest statute.

-But why, My Love, talk to me in such strong terms; every word of which cuts me to the very soul? You know, a hint, the slightest signification of your wish, is to me a sacred command.

-Be reconciled, My Angel, to your God, your self and me; and I pledge you Sylvander's honor, an oath I dare say you will trust without reserve, that you shall never more have reason to complain of his conduct.

-Now, my Love, do not wound our next meeting with any averted looks or restrained caresses: I have marked the line of conduct, a line I know exactly to your taste, and which I will inviolably keep; but do not you show the least inclination to make boundaries: seeming distrust, where you know you may confide, is a cruel sin against Sensibility.-

"Delicacy, you know it, was which won me to you at once-"take care you do not loosen the dearest most sacred tie that unites us" Clarinda, I would not have stung your soul, I would not have bruised your spirit, as that harsh crucifying, "Take care," did mine; no, not to have gained heaven! Let me again appeal to your dear Self, if Sylvander, even when he seemingly half-transgressed the laws of Decorum, if he did not shew more chastised, trembling, faultering delicacy, than the MANY of the world do in keeping these laws.-

O Love and Sensibility, ye have conspired against My Peace! I love to madness, and I feel to torture! Clarinda, how can I forgive myself, that I ever have touched a single chord in your bosom with pain! would I do it willingly? Would any consideration, any gratification make me do so?

O, did you love like me, you would not, you could not deny or put off a meeting with the Man who adores you; who would die a thousands deaths before he would injure you; and who must soon bid you a long farewell!-

I had proposed bringing my bosom friend, Mr Ainslie, tomorrow evening, at his strong request, to see you; as he only has time to stay with us about ten minutes, for an engagement; but-I shall hear from you: this afternoon, for mercy's sake! for till I hear from you I am wretched.-O Clarinda, the tie that binds me to thee, is entwisted, incorporated with my dearest threads of life!

Sylvander

II

"Unlavish Wisdom never works in vain"..!

I have been tasking my reason, Clarinda, why a woman, who for native genius, poignant wit, strength of mind, generous sincerity of soul, and the sweetest female tenderness, is without a peer; and whose personal charms have few, very, very few parallels, among her sex; why, or how she should fall to the blessed lot of a poor hairumscairum Poet, whom Fortune has kept for her particular use to wreak her temper on, whenever she was in ill-humour.

One time I conjectured that as Fortune is the most capricious jade ever known; she may have taken, not a fit of remorse, a paroxysm of whim, to raise the poor devil out of the mire, where he had so often and so conveniently served her as a stepping-stone, and give him the most glorious boon she ever had in her gift, merely for the maggot's sake, to see how his fool head and his fool heart will bear it.

At other times I was vain enough to think that Nature, who has a great deal to say with Fortune, had given the coquettish goddess some such hint as, "Here is a paragon of Female Excellence, whose equal, in all my former conposltions, I never was lucky enough to hit on, and despair of ever doing so again; you have cast her rather in the shades of life; there is a certain Poet, of my making; amongst your frolicks, it would not be amiss to attach him to this master-piece of my hand, to give her that immortality amongst mankind which no woman of any age ever more deserv'd, and which few Rhymesters of this age are better able to confer."

Evening, 9 o'clock I am here, absolutely unfit to finish my letter-pretty hearty after a bowl, which has been constantly plied since dinner, till this moment.

I have been with Mr. Schetki, the musician, and he has set it finely. -1 have no distinct ideas of any thing, but that I have drunk your health twice tonight, and that you are all my soul holds dear in this world.-

Sylvander

LORD BYRON

to Lady Caroline Lamb

August 1812

My dearest Caroline,

If tears, which you saw & know I am not apt to shed, if the agitation in which I parted from you, agitation which you must have perceived through the whole of this most nervous nervous affair, did not commence till the moment of leaving you approached, if all that I have said & done, & am still but too ready to say & do, have not sufficiently proved what my real feelings are & must be ever towards you, my love, I have no other proof to offer.

God knows I wish you happy, & when I quit you, or rather when you from a sense of duty to your husband & mother quit me, you shall acknowledge the truth of what I again promise & vow, that no other in word or deed shall ever hold the place in my affection which is & shall be most sacred to you, till I am nothing.

I never knew till that moment, the madness of -- my dearest & most beloved friend -- I cannot express myself -- this is no time for words -- but I shall have a pride, a melancholy pleasure, in suffering what you yourself can hardly conceive -- for you don not know me. -- I am now about to go out with a heavy heart, because -- my appearing this Evening will stop any absurd story which the events of today might give rise to -- do you think now that I am cold & stern, & artful -- will even others think so, will your mother even -- that mother to whom we must indeed sacrifice much, more much more on my part, than she shall ever know or can imagine.

"Promises not to love you" ah Caroline it is past promising -- but shall attribute all concessions to the proper motive -- & never cease to feel all that you have already witnessed -- & more than can ever be known but to my own heart -- perhaps to yours -- May God protect forgive & bless you -- ever & even more than ever.

yr. most attached

BYRON

P.S. -- These taunts which have driven you to this -- my dearest Caroline -- were it not for your mother & the kindness of all your connections, is there anything on earth or heaven would have made me so happy as to have made you mine long ago? & not less now than then, but more than ever at this time -- you know I would with pleasure give up all here & all beyond the grave for you -- & in refraining from this -- must my motives be misunderstood --? I care not who knows this -- what use is made of it -- it is you & to you only that they owe yourself, I was and am yours, freely & most entirely, to obey, to honour, love --& fly with you when, where, & how you yourself might & may determine.

WINSTON CHURCHILL

to Clementine Churchill

January 23, 1935

My darling Clemmie,

In your letter from Madras you wrote some words very dear to me, about my having enriched your life. I cannot tell you what pleasure this gave me, because I always feel so overwhelmingly in your debt, if there can be accounts in love.... What it has been to me to live all these years in your heart and companionship no phrases can convey. Time passes swiftly, but is it not joyous to see how great and growing is the treasure we have gathered together, amid the storms and stresses of so many eventful and to millions tragic and terrible years?

Your loving husband (Winston Churchill)

PIERRE CURIE

to Marie Curie

August 10, 1894

Nothing could have given me greater pleasure that to get news of you. The prospect of remaining two months without hearing about you had been extremely disagreeable to me: that is to say, your little note was more than welcome.

I hope you are laying up a stock of good air and that you will come back to us in October. As for me, I think I shall not go anywhere; I shall stay in the country, where I spend the whole day in front of my open window or in the garden.

We have promised each other — haven't we? — to be at least great friends. If you will only not change your mind! For there are no promises that are binding; such things cannot be ordered at will. It would be a fine thing, just the same, in which I hardly dare believe, to pass our lives near each other, hypnotized by our dreams: your patriotic dream, our humanitarian dream, and our scientific dream. Of all those dreams the last is, I believe, the only legitimate one. I mean by that that we are powerless to change the social order and, even if we were not, we should not know what to do; in taking action, no matter in what direction, we should never be sure of not doing more harm than good, by retarding some inevitable evolution. From the scientific point of view, on the contrary, we may hope to do something; the ground is solider here, and any discovery that we may make, however small, will remain acquired knowledge.

See how it works out: it is agreed that we shall be great friends, but if you leave France in a year it would be an altogether too Platonic friendship, that of two creatures who would never see each other again. Wouldn't it be better for you to stay with me? I know that this question angers you, and that you don't want to speak of it again — and then, too, I feel so thoroughly unworthy of you from every point of view.

I thought of asking your permission to meet you by chance in Fribourg. But you are staying there, unless I am mistaken, only one day, and on that day you will of course belong to our friends the Kovalskis.

Believe me your very devoted

Peirre Curie

NATHANIEL HAWTHORNE

to Sophia A. Peabody

Boston, April 2^{d}, 1839

Mine own Dove,

I have been sitting by my fireside ever since teatime, till now it is
past eight o'clock; and have been musing and dreaming about a
thousand things, with every one of which, I do believe, some
nearer or remoter thought of you was intermingled. I should
have begun this letter earlier in the evening, but was afraid that
some intrusive idler would thrust himself between us, and so the
sacredness of my letter would be partly lost;—for I feel as if my
letters were sacred, because they are written from my spirit to
your spirit. I wish it were possible to convey them to you by
other than earthly messengers—to convey them directly into your
heart, with the warmth of mine still lingering in them. When we
shall be endowed with our spiritual bodies, I think they will be
so constituted, that we may send thoughts and feelings any
distance, in no time at all, and transfuse them warm and fresh
into the consciousness of those whom we love. Oh what a bliss it
would be, at this moment; if I could be conscious of some purer
feeling, some more delicate sentiment, some lovelier fantasy,
than could possibly have had its birth in my own nature, and
therefore be aware that my Dove was thinking through my mind
and feeling through my heart! Try—some evening when you are
alone and happy, and when you are most conscious of loving me
and being loved by me—and see if you do not possess this power
already. But, after all, perhaps it is not wise to intermix fantastic
ideas with the reality of our affection. Let us content ourselves to

be earthly creatures, and hold communion of spirit in such modes as are ordained to us—by letters (dipping our pens as deep as may be into our hearts) by heartfelt words, when they can be audible; by glances—through which medium spirits do really seem to talk in their own language—and by holy kisses, which I do think have something supernatural in them.

And now good night, my beautiful Dove. I do not write any more at present, because there are three more whole days before this letter will visit you: and I desire to talk with you, each of those three days. Your letter did not come today. Even if it should not come tomorrow, I shall not imagine that you forget me or neglect me, but shall heave two or three sighs, and measure salt and coal so much the more diligently. Good night; and if I have any power, at this distance, over your spirit, it shall be exerted to make you sleep like a little baby, till the "Harper of the Golden Dawn" arouse you. Then you must finish that ode. But do, if you love me, sleep.

April 3d. No letter, my dearest; and if one comes tomorrow I shall not receive it till Friday, nor perhaps then; because I have a cargo of coal to measure in East Cambridge, and cannot go to the Custom House till the job is finished. If you had known this, I think you would have done your [best] possible to send me a letter today. Doubtless you have some good reason for omitting it. I was invited to dine at Mr. Hooper's; with your sister Mary; and the notion came into my head, that perhaps you would be there,—and though I knew that it could not be so, yet I felt as if it might. But just as I was going home from the Custom House to dress, came an abominable person to say that a measurer was wanted forthwith at East Cambridge; so over I hurried, and found that, after all, nothing would be done till tomorrow morning at sunrise. In the meantime, I had lost my dinner, and all other pleasures that had awaited me at Mr. Hooper's; so that I came back in very ill humor, and do not mean to be very good-natured again, till my Dove shall nestle upon my heart again, either in her own sweet person, or by her image in a letter. But your image will be with me, long before the letter comes. It will flit around me while I am measuring coal, and will peep over my shoulder to see whether I keep a correct account, and will smile to hear my bickerings with the black-faced demons in the vessel's hold, (they look like the forge-men in Retsch's Fridolin) and will soothe and mollify me amid all the pester and plague that is in store for me tomorrow. Not that I would avoid this pester and plague, even if it were in my power to do so. I need such training, and ought to have undergone it long ago. It will give my character a healthy hardness as regards the world; while it will leave my heart as soft—as fit for a Dove to rest upon—as it is now, or ever was. Good night again, gentle Dove. I must leave a little space for tomorrow's record; and moreover, it is almost time that I were asleep, having to get up in the dusky dawn. Did you yield to my conjurations, and sleep well last night? Well then, I throw the same spell over you tonight.

April 4th.   past 9 P.M. I came home late in the afternoon, very tired, sunburnt and sea-flushed, having walked or sat on the deck of a schooner ever since sunrise. Nevertheless, I purified myself from the sable stains of my profession—stains which I share in common with chimney sweepers—and then hastened to the Custom House to get your letter—for I *knew* there was one there awaiting me, and now I thank you with my whole heart, and will straight way go to sleep. Do you the same.

April 5th. Your yesterday's letter is received, my beloved Sophie. I have no time to answer it: but, like all your communications, personal or written, it is the sunshine of my life. I have been busy all day, and am now going to see your sister Mary—and I hope, Elizabeth. Mr. Pickens is going with me.

HENRY VIII OF FRANCE

to Anne Boleyn

MY MISTRESS & FRIEND, my heart and I surrender ourselves into your hands, beseeching you to hold us commended to your favour, and that by absence your affection to us may not be lessened: for it were a great pity to increase our pain, of which absence produces enough and more than I could ever have thought could be felt, reminding us of a point in astronomy which is this: the longer the days are, the more distant is the sun, and nevertheless the hotter; so is it with our love, for by absence we are kept a distance from one another, and yet it retains its fervour, at least on my side; I hope the like on yours, assuring you that on my part the pain of absence is already too great for me; and when I think of the increase of that which I am forced to suffer, it would be almost intolerable, but for the firm hope I have of your unchangeable affection for me: and to remind you of this sometimes, and seeing that I cannot be personally present with you, I now send you the nearest thing I can to that, namely, my picture set in a bracelet, with the whole of the device, which you already know, wishing myself in their place, if it should please you. This is from the hand of your loyal servant and friend,

H. R.

VICTOR HUGO

to Adele Foucher

My dearest,

When two souls, which have sought each other for,

however long in the throng, have finally found each other ...a union, fiery and pure as they themselves are... begins on earth and continues forever in heaven.

This union is love, true love, ... a religion, which deifies the loved one, whose life comes from devotion and passion, and for which the greatest sacrifices are the sweetest delights.

This is the love which you inspire in me... Your soul is made to love with the purity and passion of angels; but perhaps it can only love another angel, in which case I must tremble with apprehension.

Yours forever,

Victor Hugo

JAMES JOYCE

to Nora Barnacle

My dear Nora,

It has just struck me. I came in at half past eleven. Since then I have been sitting in an easy chair like a fool. I could do nothing. I hear nothing but your voice. I am like a fool hearing you call me 'Dear.' I offended two men today by leaving them coolly. I wanted to hear your voice, not theirs.

When I am with you I leave aside my contemptuous, suspicious nature. I wish I felt your head on my shoulder. I think I will go to bed.

I have been a half-hour writing this thing. Will you write something to me? I hope you will. How am I to sign myself? I won't sign anything at all, because I don't know what to sign myself.

FRANZ LISZT

to Countess Marie D'Agoult

Thursday morning 1834

My heart overflows with emotion and joy! I do not know what heavenly languor, what infinite pleasure permeates it and burns me up. It is as if I had never loved!!! Tell me whence these uncanny disturbances spring, these inexpressible foretastes of delight, these divine, tremors of love. Oh! all this can only spring from you, sister, angel, woman, Marie! All this can only be, is surely nothing less than a gentle ray streaming from your fiery soul, or else some secret poignant teardrop which you have long since left in my breast.

My God, my God, never force us apart, take pity on us! But what am I saying? Forgive my weakness, how couldst Thou divide us! Thou wouldst have nothing but pity for us...No no! It is not in vain that our flesh and our souls quicken and become immortal through Thy Word, which cries out deep within us Father, Father...out Thy hand to us, that our broken hearts seek their refuge in Thee...O! we thank, bless and praise Thee, O God, for all that Thou has given us, and all that Thou hast prepared for us....

This is to be -- to be!

Marie! Marie!

Oh let me repeat that name a hundred times, a thousand times over; for three days now it has lived within me, oppressed me, set me afire. I am not writing to you, no, I am close beside you. I see you, I hear you. Eternity in your arms... Heaven, Hell, everything, all is within you, redoubled... Oh! Leave me free to rave in my delirium. Drab, tame, constricting reality is no longer enough for me. We must live our lives to the full, loving and suffering to extremes!...

Franz

JACK LONDON

to Anna Strunsky

Dear Anna:

Did I say that the human might be filed in categories? Well, and if I did, let me qualify -- not all humans. You elude me. I cannot place you, cannot grasp you. I may boast that of nine out of ten, under given circumstances, I can forecast their action; that of nine out of ten, by their word or action, I may feel the pulse of their hearts. But of the tenth I despair. It is beyond me. You are that tenth.

Were ever two souls, with dumb lips, more incongruously matched! We may feel in common -- surely, we oftimes do -- and when we do not feel in common, yet do we understand; and yet we have no common tongue. Spoken words do not come to us. We are unintelligible. God must laugh at the mummery.

The one gleam of sanity through it all is that we are both large temperamentally, large enough to often understand. True, we often understand but in vague glimmering ways, by dim perceptions, like ghosts, which, while we doubt, haunt us with their truth. And still, I, for one, dare not believe; for you are that tenth which I may not forecast.

Am I unintelligible now? I do not know. I imagine so. I cannot find the common tongue.

Large temperamentally -- that is it. It is the one thing that brings us at all in touch. We have, flashed through us, you and I, each a bit of universal, and so we draw together. And yet we are so different.

I smile at you when you grow enthusiastic? It is a forgivable smile -- nay, almost an envious smile. I have lived twenty-five years of repression. I learned not to be enthusiastic. It is a hard lesson to forget. I begin to forget, but it is so little. At the best, before I die, I cannot hope to forget all or most. I can exult, now that I am learning, in little things, in other things; but of my things, and secret things doubly mine, I cannot, I cannot. Do I make myself intelligible? Do you hear my voice? I fear not. There are poseurs. I am the most successful of them all.

Jack

WOLFGANG MOZART

to Constanze Mozart

DEAREST, MOST BELOVED LITTLE WIFE!

What? Still in Dresden? Yes, my love. Well, I shall tell you everything as minutely as possible. On Monday, April 1 3th, after breakfasting with the Neumanns we all went to the Court chapel. The mass was by Naumann, who conducted it himself, and very poor stuff it was. We were in an oratory opposite the orchestra. All of a sudden Neumann nudged me and introduced me to Herr von Konig, who is the Directeur des Plaisirs (of the melan choly plaisirs of the Elector). He was extremely nice and when he asked me whether I should like His Highness to hear me, I replied that it would indeed be a great privilege, but that, as I was not travelling alone, I could not prolong my stay. So we left It at that. My princely travelling companion invited the Neumanns and Madame Duschek to lunch. While we were at table a message came that I was to play at court on the following day, Tuesday, April 1 4th, at half past five in the evening. That is some thing quite out of the ordinary for Dresden, for it is usually very difficult to get a hearing, and you know that I never thought of performing at court here. We had arranged a quartet among ourselves at the Hotel de Pologne.

So we performed it in the Chapel with Anton Teiber (who, as you know, is organist here) and with Herr Kraft, Prince Esterhazy's violoncellist, who is here with his son. At this little concert I introduced the trio which I wrote for Herr von Puchberg and it was played quite decently. Madame Duschek sang a number of arias from " Figaro" and "Don Giovanni". The next day I played at court my new concerto in D, and on the following morn ing, Wednesday, April 15th, I received a very handsome snuff-box. Then we lunched with the Russian Ambassador, to whom I played a great deal. After lunch we agreed to have some organ playing and drove to the church at four o'clock Naumann was there too. At this point you must know that a certain Hassler, who is organist at Erfurt, is in Dresden. Well, he too was there. He was a pupil of a pupil of Bach's.

His forte is the organ and the clavier (clavichord). Now people here think that because I come from Vienna, I am quite unacquainted with this style and mode of playing. Well, I sat down at the organ and played. Prince Lichnowsky, who knows Hassler very well, after some difficulty persuaded him to play also. This Hassler's chief excellence on the organ consists in his foot- work, which, since the pedals are graded here, is not so very wonderful. Moreover, he has done no more than commit to memory the harmony and modulations of old Sebastian Bach and is not capable of executing a fugue properly; and his playing is not thorough. Thus he is far from being an Albrechtsbergen After that we decided to go back to the Russian Ambassador's, so that Hassler might hear me on the fortepiano. He played too. I consider Mile Aurnhammer as good a player on the fortepiano as he is, so you can imagine that he has begun to sink very considerably in my estimation. After that we went to the opera, which is truly wretched. Do you know who is one of the singers? Why Rosa Manservisi. You can picture her delight at seeing me. But the leading woman singer, Madame Allegranti, is far better than Madame Ferraresi, which, I admit, is not saying very much. When the opera was over we went home. Then came the happiest of all moments for me. I found a letter from you, that letter which I had longed for so ardently, my darling, my beloved! Madame Duschek and the Neu manns were with me as usual. But I immediately went off in triumph to my room, kissed the letter countless times before breaking the seal, and then devoured it rather than read it. I stayed in my room a long time; for I could not read it or kiss it often enough. When I rejoined the com pany, the Neumanns asked me whether I had had a letter from you, and when I said that I had, they all congratu lated me most heartily as every day I had been lament ing that I had not yet heard from you. They are delightful people. Now for your dear letter. You shall receive by the next post an account of what will have taken place here up to the time of our departure.

Dear little wife, I have a number of requests to make. I beg you

(1) not to be melancholy,

(2) to take care of your health and to beware of the spring breezes,

(3) not to go out walking alone and preferably not to go out walking at all,

(4) to feel absolutely assured of my love. Up to the present I have not written a single letter to you without placing your dear portrait before me,

(5) I beg you in your conduct not only to be careful of your honour and mine but also to consider appearances. Do not be angry with me for asking this. You ought to love me even more for thus valuing our honour.

(6) and lastly I beg you to send me more details in your letters, I should very much like to know whether our brother-in-law Hofer came to see us the day after my departure? Whether he comes very often, as he promised me he would? Whether the Langes come sometimes? Whether progress is being made with the portrait? What sort of life you are leading? All these things are naturally of great interest to me

Now farewell, dearest, most beloved! Please remember that every night before going to bed I talk to your portrait for a good half hour and do the same when I awake. We are leaving on the 18th, the day after tomorrow. So continue to write to Berlin, Poste Restante.

O Stru! Stri! I kiss and squeeze you 1095060437082 times (now you can practise your pronunciation) and am ever your most faithful husband and friend

W. A. MOZART

ROBERT PEARY

to Josephine Peary

August 17, 1908

S.S. Roosevelt,

My Darling Josephine: Am nearly through with my writing. Am brain weary with the thousand and one imperative details and things to think of. Everything thus far has gone well, too well I am afraid, and I am (solely on general principles) somewhat suspicious of the future. The ship is in better shape than before; the party and crew are apparently harmonious; I have 21 Eskimo men (against 23 last time) but the total of men women and children is only 50 as against 67 before owing to a more careful selection as to children... I have landed supplies here, and leave two men ostensibly on behalf of Cook.

As a matter of fact I have established here the sub-base which last I established at Victoria Head, as a precaution in event of loss of the Roosevelt either going up this fall or coming down next summer. In some respects this is an advantage as on leaving here there is nothing to delay me or keep me from taking either side of the Channel going up. the conditions give me entire control of the situation...

You have been with me constantly, sweetheart. At Kangerdlooksoah I looked repeatedly at Ptarmigan Island and thought of the time we camped there. At Nuuatoksoah I landed where we were. And on the 11th we passed the mouth of Bowdoin Bay in brilliant weather, and as long as I could I kept my eyes on Anniversary Lodge. We have been great chums dear. Tell Marie to remember what I told her, tell "Mister Man" [Robert Peary, Jr.] to remember "straight and strong and clean and honest", obey orders, and never forget that Daddy put "Mut" in his charge till he himself comes back to take her. In fancy I kiss your dear eyes and lips and cheeks sweetheart; and dream of you and my children, and my home till I come again. Kiss my babies for me. Aufwiedersehen.

Love, Love, Love. Your Bert

EDGAR ALLEN POE

to Frances Sargent Osgood

For her this rhyme is penned, whose luminous eyes,

Brightly expressive as the twins of Leda,

Shall find her own sweet name, that nestling lies

Upon the page, enwrapped from every reader.

Search narrowly the lines! they hold a treasure

Devine - a talisman - an amulet

That must be worn at heart. Search well the measure -

The words - the syllables! Do not forget

The trivialest point, or you may lose your labor

And yet there is in this no Gordian knot

Which one might not undo without a sabre,

If one could merely comprehend the plot.

Enwritten upon the leaf where now are peering

Eyes scintillating soul, there lie perdus

Three eloquent words oft uttered in the hearing

Of poets, by poets - as the name is a poet's, too,

Its letters, although naturally lying

Like the knight Pinto-Mendez Ferdinando-

Still form a synonym for Truth - Cease trying!

You will not read the riddle, though you do the best you can do.

SIR WALTER RALEIGH

to Elizabeth Raleigh

You shall now receive (my dear wife) my last words in these my last lines. My love I send you that you may keep it when I am dead, and my counsel that you may remember it when I am no more.

I would not by my will present you with sorrows (dear Besse) let them go to the grave with me and be buried in the dust. And seeing that it is not God's will that I should see you any more in this life, bear it patiently, and with a heart like thy self.

First, I send you all the thanks which my heart can conceive, or my words can rehearse for your many travails, and care taken for me, which though they have not taken effect as you wished, yet my debt to

you is not the less; but pay it I never shall in this world.

Secondly, I beseech you for the love you bear me living, do not hide your self many days, but by your travails seek to help your miserable fortunes and the right of your poor child. Thy mourning cannot avail me, I am but dust...

Remember your poor child for his father's sake, who chose you, and loved you in his happiest times. Get those letters which I wrote to the Lords, wherein I sued for my life; God is my witness it was for you and yours that I desired life, but it is true that I disdained my self for begging of it: for know it that your son is the son of a true man, and one who in his own respect despiseth death and all his misshapen and ugly forms.

I cannot write much, God he knows how hardly I steal this time while others sleep, and it is also time that I should separate my thoughts from the world. Beg my dead body which living was denied thee; and either lay it at Sherburne or in Exeter Church, by my Father and Mother; I can say no more, time and death call me away....

Written with the dying hand of sometimes they Husband, but now alas overthrown. Yours that was, but now not my own.

ROBERT SCHUMANN

to Clara Wieck

Clara,

How happy your last letters have made me -- those since Christmas Eve! I should like to call you by all the endearing epithets, and yet I can find no lovelier word than the simple word 'dear,' but there is a particular way of saying it. My dear one, then, I have wept for joy to think that you are mine, and often wonder if I deserve you.

One would think that no one man's heart and brain could stand all the things that are crowded into one day. Where do these thousands of thoughts, wishes, sorrows, joys and hopes come from? Day in, day out, the procession goes on. But how light-hearted I was yesterday and the day before! There shone out of your letters so noble a spirit, such faith, such a wealth of love!

What would I not do for love of you, my own Clara! The knights of old were better off; they could go through fire or slay dragons to win their ladies, but we of today have to content ourselves with more prosaic methods, such as smoking fewer cigars, and the like. After all, though, we can love, knights or no knights; and so, as ever, only the times change, not men's hearts...

You cannot think how your letter has raised and strengthened me... You are splendid, and I have much more reason to be proud of you than you of me. I have made up my mind, though, to read all your wishes in your face. Then you will think, even though

53

you don't say it, that your Robert is a really good sort, that he is entirely yours, and he loves you more than words can say.

You shall indeed have cause to think so in the happy future. I still see you as you looked in your little cap that last evening. I still hear you call me du. Clara, I heard nothing of what you said but that du. Don't you remember?

But I see you in many another unforgettable guise. Once you were in a black dress, going to the theatre with Emilia List; it was during our separation. I know you will not have forgotten; it is vivid with me. Another time you were walking in the Thomasgasschen with an umbrella up, and you avoided me in desperation. And yet another time, as you were putting on your hat after a concert, our eyes happened to meet, and yours were full of the old unchanging love.

I picture you in all sorts of ways, as I have seen you since. I did not look at you much, but you charmed me so immeasurably... Ah, I can never praise you enough for yourself or for your love of me, which I don't really deserve.

Robert

DYLAN THOMAS

to Caitlin Thomas

Caitlin Caitlin Caitlin my love my love, where are you & where am I and why haven't you written and I love you every second of every hour of every day & night. I love you, Caitlin. In all the hotel bedrooms I've been in in this two weeks, I've waited for you all the time.

She can't be long now, I say to my damp miserable self, any minute now she'll be coming into the room: the most beautiful woman on the earth, and she is mine, & I am hers, until the end of the earth and long long after. Caitlin, I love you. Have you forgotten me? Do you hate me?

Why don't you write? Two weeks may seem a small time but to me it's old as the hills & deep as my worship of you....

And in two weeks I've travelled all over the stinking place, even into the deep South: in 14 days I've given 14 readings... I'm coming back, by plane, on the 26th of May, & will tell you later just when the plane arrives. Will you meet me in London?....

I love you, I want you, it's burning hell without you. I don't want to see anybody or talk to anybody, I'm lost without you. I love your body & your soul & your eyes & your hair & your voice & the way you walk & talk. And that's all I can see now: you moving, in a light...

I've been to foul Washington; I've been to Virginia & North Carolina and Pennsylvania & Syracuse....and now I'm back in New

York, for two days, in the same room we had... I am profoundly in love with you, the only profundity I know. Every day's dull torture, every night burning for you ...

I LOVE you.

MARK TWAIN (SAMUEL CLEMENS)

to Olivia Langdon

Livy dear,

I have already mailed to-day's letter, but I am so proud of my privilege of writing the dearest girl in the world whenever I please, that I must add a few lines if only to say I love you, Livy. For I do love you, Livy...as the dew loves the flowers; as the birds love the sunshine; as the wavelets love the breeze; as mothers love their first-born; as memory loves old faces; as the yearning tides love the moon; as the angels love the pure in heart...

Take my kiss and my benediction, and try to be reconciled to the fact that I am

Yours forever,

Sam

.....

P.S.– I have read this letter over and it is flippant and foolish and puppyish. I wish I had gone to bed when I got back, without writing. You said I must never tear up a letter after writing it to you and so I send it. Burn it, Livy, I did not think I was writing so clownishly and shabbily. I was in much too good a humor for sensible letter writing

VOLTAIRE

to Catherine Olympe Dunoyer

I am a prisoner here in the name of the King; they can take my life, but not the love that I feel for you. Yes, my adorable mistress, to-night I shall see you, if I had to put my head on the block to do it. For heaven's sake, do not speak to me in such disastrous terms as you write; you must live and be cautious; beware of Madame your mother as of your worst enemy.

What do I say?

Beware of everybody; trust no one; keep yourself in readiness, as soon as the moon is visible; I shall leave the hotel incognito, take a carriage or a chaise, we shall drive like the wind to Sheveningen; I shall take paper and ink with me; we shall write our letters. If you love me, reassure yourself; and call all your strength and presence of mind to your aid; do not let your mother notice anything, try to have your pictures, and be assured that the menace of the greatest tortures will not prevent me to serve you. No, nothing has the power to part me from you; our love is based upon virtue, and will last as long as our lives.

Adieu, there is nothing that I will not brave for your sake; you deserve much more than that.

Adieu, my dear heart!

WOODROW WILSON

to Edith Wilson

My noble, incomparable Edith,

I do not know how to express or analyze the conflicting emotions that have surged like a storm through my heart all night long. I only know that first and foremost in all my thoughts has been the glorious confirmation you gave me last night — without effort, unconsciously, as of course — of all I have ever thought of your mind and heart.

You have the greatest soul, the noblest nature, the sweetest, most loving heart I have ever known, and my love, my reverence, my admiration for you, you have increased in one evening as I should have thought only a lifetime of intimate, loving association could have increased them.

You are more wonderful and lovely in my eyes than you ever were before; and my pride and joy and gratitude that you should love me with such a perfect love are beyond all expression, except in some great poem which I cannot write.

Your own,

Woodrow

Made in the USA
Middletown, DE
26 December 2014